Angelina Ballerina's
Storybook Treasury

Angelina
Ballerina

Published by Pleasant Company Publications
Stories first published in Great Britain by Penguin Books Ltd., 2002
© 2003 Helen Craig Limited and Katharine Holabird
Based on the text by Katharine Holabird and the illustrations by Helen Craig
From the scripts by Laura Beaumont, Mellie Buse, Dave Ingham, Sally-Ann Lever,
James Mason, Jan Page, and Barbara Slade

The Angelina Ballerina name and character and the dancing Angelina logo are trademarks of
HIT Entertainment PLC, Katharine Holabird, and Helen Craig. ANGELINA is registered in the U.K.
and Japan. The dancing Angelina logo is registered in the U.K.

Visit our Web site at **www.americangirl.com** and
Angelina's very own site at **www.angelinaballerina.com**

Printed in China

04 05 06 07 08 09 10 C&C 10 9 8 7 6 5 4 3

Library of Congress Cataloging-in-Publication Data
Angelina Ballerina's storybook treasury / based on the classic picture books
by Katharine Holabird and Helen Craig.
p. cm.
"Angelina Ballerina."
Summary: Angelina Ballerina learns lessons about friendship, family, and fairness as she dances
her way through six stories: "Angelina and the butterfly," "The costume ball," "Two mice in a boat,"
"Angelina and the rag doll," "Angelina in the wings," and "A day at the fair."
ISBN 1-58485-761-7 (hc)
[1. Mice—Fiction. 2. Ballet dancing—Fiction.] I. Holabird, Katharine. II. Craig, Helen, ill.
III. Angelina Ballerina (Television program)
PZ7.A582355 2003
[E]—dc22 2003059657

Angelina™ Ballerina

Angelina Ballerina's Storybook Treasury

Based on the classic picture books by Katharine Holabird and Helen Craig

PLEASANT COMPANY PUBLICATIONS™

Angelina and the Butterfly

Story adapted by Katharine Holabird
from the script by Sally-Ann Lever

BASED ON THE CLASSIC PICTURE BOOKS
BY KATHARINE HOLABIRD AND HELEN CRAIG

"What a perfect day!" Angelina smiled at her best friend, Alice.
Angelina always loved to go on Miss Lilly's special picnics in
Big Wood with her friends from ballet school, and today even her
little cousin, Henry, was invited to join in the fun.

The hungry mouselings very quickly ate all the delicious pies and cakes. Then Angelina and her friends jumped up to play.

"Oh, look!" cried Angelina, as a large pink butterfly landed on her paw. "Isn't he beautiful?"

Everyone crowded around to admire the lovely butterfly.

"Can I hold him, Angelina?" begged Henry.

"Absolutely not!" said Angelina. "Look! He's damaged his leg. You might hurt him." She showed her friends the butterfly's twisted leg.

"I'm going to have to look after him myself," Angelina declared. And she carried the hurt butterfly very carefully all the way back to her cottage, with Henry and Alice following behind.

"I'm calling my butterfly Arthur," Angelina told her parents. "King of all the flowers, trees, and sky."

Mr. Mouseling found Arthur a large glass jar, and Mrs. Mouseling brought Arthur some leaves.

"Please can I put Arthur in the jar?" Henry asked, jumping up and down with excitement.

Angelina shook her head. "You might drop him," she said as she gently put Arthur in the jar herself. "And now he needs to stay in his house and rest," Angelina added firmly.

The next morning when they looked in the jar, Arthur was beating his wings against the glass.

"Arthur's flying!" cried Henry happily.

"Maybe he wants to go back to his family," said Alice.

But Angelina knew better. "This is his home now," she reminded them.

Angelina and Alice went to have their breakfast, while Henry sneaked back into the room to have another peek at Arthur. Very carefully, he lifted the lid off the jar for a better look. PING!

The lid sailed into the air, and Arthur flew out of the jar.

"Oh no!" cried Henry. "Come back, Arthur!"

Henry chased the butterfly around and around Angelina's room, but Arthur was too fast for him.

Then, just as Angelina came through the door to see what all the noise was about, Arthur flew out the window and disappeared.

"HENRY!" cried Angelina.

"I'm sorry!" wailed Henry. "It was an accident."

"We have to find Arthur!" Angelina shouted, and she raced out the door with Henry just behind her.

The two mouselings ran up and down the cobbled streets of Chipping Cheddar, looking everywhere and asking everyone, but no one had seen a pink butterfly. Angelina was so tired, she sat down and burst into tears. "Arthur's gone forever," she sobbed.

Henry tried to think of something nice to say. "Maybe Arthur's gone back to Big Wood," he whispered.

Angelina jumped to her feet. "That's it!" she cried, and she raced off down the road again, with Henry running as fast as he could to catch up.

They reached the woods just as it was getting dark. Angelina thought she saw something pink in the bushes and ran to catch it. "ARTHUUURRR!" she shouted. But Angelina's feet got tangled in the creepers. Then she tripped over a log and fell head over heels into a deep, dark pit.

Henry rushed after her and bravely reached down to save her when . . . OOPS! He tumbled into the pit himself and landed with a thump next to Angelina.

"Ouch!" he cried.

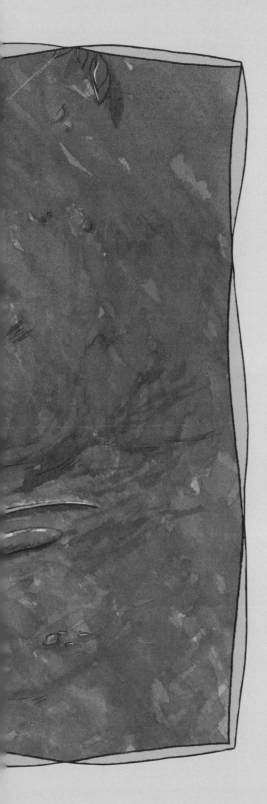

It was cold and muddy down in the pit, and much too deep for them to climb out.

"I'm scared!" Henry whimpered.

Suddenly Angelina wasn't angry with Henry anymore, and she gave him a cuddle. "Don't worry, Henry," said Angelina, even though she felt worried, too.

"I'm really sorry about losing Arthur," Henry sniffed in a tiny voice.

"It's okay, Henry," Angelina forgave him. "I know you didn't mean to lose him."

As the hours ticked by, everyone in the village came to join the search for the two lost mouselings.

"They're not at my house," panted Alice.

"And they're not down by Miller's Pond," sighed William.

"Oh, where could they be?" cried Miss Lilly, wiping away her tears.

Suddenly Alice looked up, and there was Arthur fluttering just over her head.

"Quick!" she shouted. "Let's follow Arthur!"

The butterfly flew off toward the woods, and everyone scrambled through the grass behind him. Before long, they could hear Angelina and Henry's shouts for help.

"Thank goodness you're alive!" cried Miss Lilly as Mr. Mouseling pulled the two mouselings out of the pit.

"But how did you find us?" asked Angelina.

"Arthur showed us the way," smiled Alice.

Everyone looked up to thank the butterfly, but Arthur was already gone. Poor Angelina burst into tears.

The next day when Henry and Alice came over, Angelina was still thinking about her butterfly.

"I don't suppose I'll ever see Arthur again," she sighed. Just then, a beautiful pink butterfly appeared and perched on the tip of her nose.

"It's Arthur!" cried Henry. "Let's put him back in the jar!"

"No!" cried out Angelina.

"But he'll fly away again," Henry whimpered.

"I know," said Angelina, "but being trapped is awful, and to be happy, butterflies need to be free."

Then Angelina waved good-bye, and Arthur fluttered back up to the sky and joined a crowd of beautifully colored dancing butterflies.

The Costume Ball

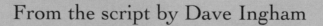

From the script by Dave Ingham

BASED ON THE CLASSIC PICTURE BOOKS
BY KATHARINE HOLABIRD AND HELEN CRAIG

It was the day of the costume ball, and Angelina hadn't been invited. "If you're going as a queen and Dad's going as a king, it makes sense that I go as a princess!" she said to Mrs. Mouseling.

"I'm sorry, Angelina," said Mrs. Mouseling patiently. "The ball is for grown-ups, not little mouselings!"

"Everyone should be allowed to go to the ball," complained Angelina to Alice later. Her friend emerged from the dress-up box wearing a hat and a dress that were far too big for her.

Alice danced until she tripped over the hem and fell on top of Angelina. "Sorry!" she giggled. "You could fit us both in this dress!"

"Yes . . ." said Angelina thoughtfully.

31

It was almost time for the costume ball to begin, and Mrs. Mouseling looked beautiful. "Mrs. Hodgepodge will be here any minute to baby-sit," she said.

"Oh, no!" groaned Angelina. "Last time she kept me awake all night with her horrible snoring!"

"I hope she doesn't bring her cabbage jelly," whispered Alice.

Mr. Mouseling came into the room dressed like a giant bee instead of a king.

"Mix-up at the costume shop!" he explained, as Angelina and Alice giggled.

Just then Mrs. Hodgepodge arrived. "Good night, you
two," said Mrs. Mouseling as she swept out the door on
Mr. Mouseling's arm. "Be good for Mrs. Hodgepodge!"

After a horrible dinner of cabbage jelly, Angelina and
Alice ran upstairs. "I wish we were at the ball," sighed
Angelina. "Would you care to dance?"

"I'd love to," said Alice with a smile.

Downstairs, Mrs. Hodgepodge had fallen asleep and was beginning to snore loudly. Angelina was trying to listen to the beautiful music drifting through the window from the ball.

"Come on, Alice!" exclaimed Angelina as she began rummaging through the dress-up box.

"Come on where?" asked Alice.

"To the costume ball, of course!"

"But what about Mrs. Hodgepodge?" whispered Alice.

"She'll be asleep for hours!" replied Angelina, tossing a hat over to Alice.

As Angelina and Alice entered the hall, they gasped.

"Wow! Look, Alice! It's wonderful!" exclaimed Angelina.
From within their disguise, the two mouselings looked around
them. Angelina wobbled on Alice's shoulders as they tottered
toward a table piled with delicious things to eat.

"All that fooood!" cried Alice.

"Careful, Alice!" whispered Angelina as Alice grabbed
a cheese ball.

"Such a wonderful party, don't you agree, my dear?"
asked a familiar voice.

It was Miss Lilly!

"Er, yes, Miss . . . miss . . . absolutely unmissable!"
stuttered Angelina in her most grown-up voice.

Luckily, just then Dr. Tuttle appeared.

"I was wondering if you'd care to dance?" he asked Miss Lilly.

"It would be a pleasure, darling!" she replied as she took his
paw. "See you later for the Whiskers Reel!" said Miss Lilly
to the mouselings as she disappeared.

"I wish someone would ask me to dance," said Angelina
glumly as she watched them make their way onto the
crowded dance floor.

Back at the Mouselings' cottage, Mrs. Hodgepodge woke up when she felt a draft. "It's coming from Angelina's room," she muttered as she went to investigate. The window was wide open.

At the ball, Angelina was desperate to dance when a voice announced, "Take your positions for the Whiskers Reel!"

"Come on, Alice!" Angelina whispered. Everyone lined up, and the music started.

As they danced, Angelina began to lose her balance on Alice's shoulders. She wobbled and bumped into her father, but luckily he didn't recognize her. Alice and Angelina stumbled into the table, and cheese balls flew everywhere as the two mouselings landed in a big, sticky heap.

Just at that moment, Mrs. Hodgepodge threw open the doors of the hall.

"There they are, those naughty little runaways!" she cried.

"Angelina!" gasped Mr. and Mrs. Mouseling.

Everyone stared at the two mouselings as they sat on the floor, surrounded by cheese balls and trying hard not to cry.

Now they were in real trouble.

Angelina and Alice were up early the next morning. There was a great deal of mess to be cleaned up in the hall.

"My back's aching! This is such hard work!" groaned Alice, mopping the floor.

"I'm so tired! Perhaps going to the ball wasn't such a good idea," sighed Angelina as she scrubbed away.

The door opened, and Mrs. Mouseling came in with
Mrs. Hodgepodge. "We've brought you something
to eat!" said Angelina's mother, smiling.

Angelina and Alice took huge bites from the delicious-
looking sandwiches.

"Oh, no!" they groaned. "Cabbage jelly!"

53

Two Mice in a Boat

From the script by Laura Beaumont

BASED ON THE CLASSIC PICTURE BOOKS
BY KATHARINE HOLABIRD AND HELEN CRAIG

It was bedtime, but Angelina wasn't tired. She'd found her father's old Miller's Pond Boat Carnival trophy.

"Oh, Dad! I'm determined to win this year," she said.

"And how are you going to decorate your boat, Angelina?" asked her father.

"Well," began Angelina, "it will be a huge white swan, with gold thrones for Alice and me, the Swan Princesses!"

"It sounds lovely, dear, but don't count on being teamed up with Alice," warned Mrs. Mouseling gently.

The next day at school, Miss Chalk announced the boat-decorating teams. "Priscilla with Penelope, Flora with William, Angelina with Sammy . . ."

"Sammy!" said Angelina, shocked.

"Angelina!" sputtered Sammy.

"Alice with Henry," continued Miss Chalk. Alice looked horrified.

"It's all about teamwork!" said Miss Chalk over the din of unhappy mice.

Angelina and Sammy lined up to collect their boat from Captain Miller.

"I wouldn't be seen dead in a sissy swan boat," muttered Sammy.

"Well, you wouldn't catch me on some stupid pirate ship!" spat Angelina. She sighed as she looked at Sammy's plans. "We're never going to agree, so we'll just have to try and . . ."

"Work together," they both muttered.

The next day, they drew a line down the middle of the boat. They decided to decorate one-half each. "Don't go over the line," warned Angelina sternly.

"Don't worry, I won't!" said Sammy.

Down near the river, Alice and Henry were decorating their boat with sweets.

"One for the boat, one for you!" they said happily, popping candies into each other's mouths.

On the day of the carnival, Angelina and Sammy got ready
early and went to try out their boat on the river.

"It floats!" cried Angelina when they eventually managed
to launch it.

The two mice turned around when they heard a rumbling noise behind them. It was the builder mouse, Mr. Ratchett.

"Nice boat you've got there!" he said. "What's she called?"

"The Swan Princess," said Angelina.

"The Pirate King!" shouted Sammy.

"That's a big name for a small boat!" chuckled Mr. Ratchett as he carried on up the road.

The mouselings jumped on board.

"I think we're sinking," said Sammy as he watched water seeping into the boat.

"I said that cannon was too heavy!" cried Swan Princess Angelina furiously.

"It's probably that stupid bird's head," muttered Pirate Sammy.

They began to throw things out of the boat as fast as they could, until there was absolutely nothing left.

"We're floating now," said Sammy.

"Downstream!" shouted Angelina desperately. "Where are the oars?"

"Over there!" cried Sammy, pointing to the oars floating away in the water.

Meanwhile, Alice and Henry had nearly finished their boat, but they'd spent quite a lot of time eating the decorations and felt a little sick!

Farther downstream, Angelina and Sammy were moving fast.

"We've got to stop!" yelled Angelina.

"I can see a tree stump up ahead!" bellowed Sammy.

"We need some rope to loop over it. Look!" Angelina had seen something.

"Vines!" they both said together.

As the little boat sped along, the two frightened mice grabbed onto the vines.

"Hold on!" shouted Sammy.

The vines broke away from the bank, and Angelina found the longest one. Angelina and Sammy both grabbed onto it just as the boat reached the tree stump.

They struggled to loop the vine over the stump and pulled themselves onto the bank.

"We have to get back to Miller's Pond!" cried a desperate Angelina.

Just then, Sammy and Angelina heard a *chug chug* behind them.

"Mr. Ratchett!" they both shouted, relieved.

At Miller's Pond, the carnival was under way. Alice and Henry were dressed as candy canes, and their boat was decorated entirely with candy wrappers!

Suddenly there was a distant chugging noise, and everybody turned to look.

It was Swan Princess Angelina and Pirate Sammy. They were floating along in the sky on the end of Mr. Ratchett's crane!

Everyone at Miller's Pond clapped and cheered as Angelina and Sammy were slowly lowered toward the water.

SPLASH! They landed a bit too close to Priscilla and
Penelope Pinkpaws' boat. It was decorated as a huge
pink ballet shoe. "Our lovely shoe!" they squeaked.
"Now it's soaking wet!"

Angelina and Sammy giggled together.

"The winners of the boat-decorating contest are Alice and
Henry," said Captain Miller a little later. "But this year's
prize for teamwork goes to Angelina and Sammy!"

Mr. Mouseling introduced Angelina to his old boating
partner—Sammy's dad! "We never won a teamwork
prize," said Mr. Watts. "We were always arguing."

"No we weren't!" replied Mr. Mouseling.

Angelina and Sammy giggled.

"YOU keep the trophy," said Angelina.

"No, you keep it," replied Sammy.

The two mouselings, and their fathers, carried on arguing and laughing until the sun went down and it was time for every tired mouse to go home to bed.

Angelina and the Rag Doll

Story adapted by Katharine Holabird
from the script by James Mason

BASED ON THE CLASSIC PICTURE BOOKS
BY KATHARINE HOLABIRD AND HELEN CRAIG

Angelina couldn't wait to tell her best friend, Alice, the exciting news.

"Miss Lilly needs a helper for the beginner's ballet class," Angelina announced proudly as they walked home together, "and she asked ME!"

The two little mouselings went to
Mrs. Thimble's General Store to buy
some sweets to celebrate.

"Don't forget my secondhand box,"
Mrs. Thimble reminded them as they
were about to leave. "Just bring
anything you don't need anymore,
and it will help a good cause."

When she got home, Angelina made a collection of all the things she'd outgrown.

"What's this?" asked Alice, holding up an old rag doll mouse in a torn tutu.

"Oh, that's Polka," said Angelina. "We used to dance together when I first started at Miss Lilly's Ballet School."

"Where did you get her?" Alice asked.

"I don't remember," said Angelina. "But I'm too grown-up for her now."

Angelina added Polka to the collection. The next morning the two mouselings carried all Angelina's old clothes and toys to the General Store, and everything went straight into Mrs. Thimble's secondhand box.

The following week, Angelina's grandpa and grandma came for tea and decided to have a look at Angelina's baby photographs. "Ahh," said Grandma, smiling. "Here's a picture of you at your first ballet lesson, with Polka."

"Do you remember the day I won Polka for you at the fair?" Grandpa asked. "And you said you'd never ever let her go."

"Y-y-yes, Grandpa," Angelina stammered, suddenly remembering.

"You called her Polka because that was the special dance we always did together," Grandpa said. "Let's see if we can still remember it."

But Angelina was already running out the door. "I'm sorry," Angelina called, "but I forgot to tell Alice something important!"

Angelina ran all the way to Alice's cottage to tell her the terrible news.

"We've got to get Polka back!" Angelina shouted. They raced off together as fast as they could to Mrs. Thimble's General Store.

The two mouselings searched in all Mrs. Thimble's secondhand boxes, but Polka was nowhere to be found.

"I'm afraid your doll's already been taken," Mrs. Thimble said.

Angelina couldn't believe that Polka was gone. She made big posters with Polka's picture on them and stuck them all around the village. But nobody brought Polka back.

Then Angelina went up and down the streets with Alice and asked about Polka at every shop and house, but the villagers just shook their heads.

Finally, Angelina and Alice went to see Miss Twitchett, who collected things for charity.

"I've just sent all the toys to the poor children in Dacovia," said Miss Twitchett.

"What am I going to do?" Angelina cried.

"At least you'll have fun helping Miss Lilly at ballet school tomorrow," Alice kindly reminded her.

Angelina couldn't let Miss Lilly down, so the next morning she put on her tutu and went to help with the ballet lessons.

Most of the little dancers were happily crowding around Miss Lilly, but one small mouseling was too shy to join in.

"Come in and sit down, Mary," said Miss Lilly, smiling. But Mary shook her head and stayed by herself in the corner, clutching an old rag doll.

Angelina looked closer—and gasped. She couldn't believe her eyes— little Mary was holding Polka!

"Excuse me, she's my . . ." Angelina stopped herself. She could see that Mary really loved Polka.

"She's a lovely doll," Angelina said with a smile. "And she loves to dance. May I show you?" Mary nodded and handed Polka to Angelina.

Angelina began to dance with Polka, the way she always used to, and little Mary smiled and forgot about feeling so shy. Soon she was laughing and dancing around and around the room with Angelina and Polka.

"Well done, darlings." Miss Lilly clapped her hands.

For the rest of the lesson, Mary followed Angelina and tried to do all the ballet exercises just the way Angelina showed her.

At the end of the morning, Angelina waited with Miss Lilly to say good-bye to all the new ballet students.

"See you next week, Mary," said Angelina.

"I hope I can be a beautiful dancer like you someday," said Mary, smiling.

"I'm sure you will," Angelina encouraged her.

Mary hugged Polka. "I'm going to call her Angelina. Is that all right?"

"Yes," said Angelina quietly. "I'd really like that."

The next time that Grandma and Grandpa came to tea, Angelina told them all about Polka and Mary.

"I loved Polka, and I'm really sorry for breaking my promise to you, Grandpa," Angelina said.

"You did a very grown-up thing," said Grandpa. "I'm really proud of you, Angelina."

Angelina gave her grandpa an enormous hug, and Mr. Mouseling started to play his fiddle.

"May I have the honor of this dance?" asked Grandpa with a bow.

Angelina curtsied. Then she and Grandpa laughed and danced around the cottage while her father played the polka, and Angelina was absolutely delighted because she still remembered every step!

Angelina in the Wings

From the script by Mellie Buse

BASED ON THE CLASSIC PICTURE BOOKS
BY KATHARINE HOLABIRD AND HELEN CRAIG

"I have wonderful news!" said Miss Lilly one day after class. "As you know, the famous Madame Zizi is to perform *The Sun Queen* at the Theater Royal. And she is coming here tomorrow with Mr. Popoff, the director, to watch our class!"

Everyone gasped with delight.

"One of the little sunbeams in the ballet has mousepox,"
Miss Lilly continued.

"Does that mean they need another sunbeam?" asked
Angelina, hardly daring to believe it.

"It does, Angelina! Indeed it does," said Miss Lilly with
a smile.

That evening at supper, Cousin Henry was running around the kitchen, playing with his windup ladybug and singing. He was very excited about Angelina being a sunbeam.

Angelina, however, was getting nervous. "Don't worry," said Mrs. Mouseling. "You'll have Henry there as your mascot!"

"WHAT!" Angelina was horrified. "I have to take Henry to the audition?"

"I'll be the best mascot ever!" said Henry, spilling his drink.
"What's a mascot?"

"Someone who brings luck," said Mrs. Mouseling cheerfully.

Angelina groaned.

The next day at class, Angelina felt very nervous.
Mr. Popoff was going to teach the lesson so that
Madame Zizi could watch the mouselings dance.
Henry sat at the side of the room, playing with his
ladybug and trying to keep still.

"Alice!" whispered Angelina to her best friend as they
began to dance. "This sunbeam is about to shine!"

As Angelina spun around the room, she hissed at Henry to sit quietly.

"Zee leetle peenk mouseling," said Madame Zizi suddenly.

"On your own, please," said Mr. Popoff.

"Enchantée!" exclaimed Madame Zizi, as she watched Angelina dance on her own.

Suddenly a fly landed on Henry's nose, and he dropped his ladybug. "Oh, no!" he cried, chasing his toy across the floor. The ladybug bumped into Angelina, and over she toppled.

"What a sweet mouseling!" said Madame Zizi, spotting Henry. "He must be our sunbeam! Zee peenk one can understudy."

"I can't believe Henry got the part!" sobbed Angelina that evening. "And I just have to stand and watch. It's so unfair!"

Alice tried to comfort her. "But when Madame Zizi sees how good you are, she's bound to make room for another sunbeam!" she said cheerily, offering Angelina a cheesy niblet.

The next day, all the sunbeams, and Angelina, danced in perfect time—except for Henry.

"Jump like Angelina!" said Mr. Popoff.

Henry tried hard, but it was very difficult for such a tiny mouse.

"Move back, Angelina!" continued Mr. Popoff. "They must
do it alone."

That evening, Angelina called Alice. "How can I get
Madame Zizi to notice me?" she cried desperately.

She watched little Henry as he danced around the room.
Mrs. Mouseling came in just as he tripped over Angelina's
ballet things, thrown carelessly on the floor. "Oh, Angelina!
I'm not your servant!" Mrs. Mouseling scolded as she
began picking things up.

Servant! thought Angelina. That's a good idea!

The next day, Angelina did everything for Madame Zizi. She ran around fetching and carrying until she was exhausted. Just before the rehearsal, she even helped with Madame Zizi's costume!

"Where is the little boy mouseling?" asked Mr. Popoff impatiently a few minutes later. "We are ready to start!" Everyone looked around.

"Here I am!" sang Henry, running onto the stage a little out of breath. He'd gotten lost backstage.

Madame Zizi swept him into her arms. "Eet is not hees fault," she said. "Angelina should have been looking after heem like I told her to!"

As she waited backstage, Angelina began to sob.
Alice tried to cheer her up.

126

Then Angelina and Alice heard Mr. Popoff's voice coming from the stage. "Zizi, we have to bring on the understudy sunbeam! The boy mouseling must go." Angelina was stunned. Poor Henry!

"Please give him another chance," Angelina cried. "I can help him. I promise!"

Madame Zizi agreed. "Yes, Popoff! You weel geev heem one more chance at the dress rehearsal tomorrow. I inseest!"

That evening, Angelina helped Henry as he struggled
with the difficult steps. "Well done!" she said. "Now
we'll try it again. Watch me!"

At last it was time for the dress rehearsal. At the theater, the sunbeams waited in their dressing room with Mr. Popoff, ready to go onstage.

Suddenly, Madame Zizi rushed in.

"Whatever is the matter, Zizi?" asked Mr. Popoff nervously.

"Disaster!" she replied. "Another one of our leetle sunbeams has zee mousepox!"

Angelina had her chance at last! The little sunbeams danced their hearts out, and at the end of the performance, they took their bows behind the famous Madame Zizi.

As the performers left the stage, the applause was deafening. Mr. and Mrs. Mouseling, Henry's parents, Alice, and Miss Lilly leaped to their feet and clapped as hard as they could.

"Oh, Henry! You were wonderful," said Angelina breathlessly.

"You were indeed perfect, Henry," said Mr. Popoff with a smile. "And it was all thanks to you, Angelina!"

The next morning, Angelina and Henry sat side by side in bed, covered in pink mousepox spots! They heard a knock on the bedroom door.

"Room service," laughed Mrs. Mouseling, popping her head around the door. "I've brought some cheesy niblets, sent by Alice, for two spectacular spotty sunbeams!"

A Day at the Fair

From the script by Barbara Slade and Jan Page

BASED ON THE CLASSIC PICTURE BOOKS
BY KATHARINE HOLABIRD AND HELEN CRAIG

"Excellent, darlings!" said Miss Lilly at the end of the dance class.

Angelina and her friend Alice rushed to get changed.

"Just think, Alice," said Angelina. "In exactly one hour, you and I will be riding on the fastest, scariest roller coaster in all of Mouseland! Hurry up, William. We'll be late for the fair!"

Angelina rushed home and counted the money in her piggy bank. "Hooray!" she said. "Just enough for cotton candy!" Scooping up the coins, she ran to the door.

Unfortunately she bumped straight into Mrs. Mouseling and little cousin Henry.

"Excuse me, young lady," said her mother. "You promised to look after Henry today."

"But I'm going to the fair!" cried Angelina.

"Great!" said Henry. "I love fairs!"

Angelina sighed and, fixing a grin on her face, took him by the paw.

At the entrance to the fair, Angelina and Henry bought
their tickets with pocket money from Mrs. Mouseling.
Then they headed straight for the rides.

"Look at the merry-go-round, Angelina! I love them.
Don't you?" asked Henry.

"No, Henry," said Angelina sniffily. "Merry-go-rounds are for babies."

"And there's a man selling balloons!" continued Henry. "Can I have a blue one? Please?"

"No, you can't, Henry! I've only got enough money left for cotton candy."

They walked across the noisy fairground until Angelina found Alice and William.

The four mouselings rushed around the colorful fairground, looking at all the different rides, until at last they came to the Ferris wheel. Henry could hardly see the top of it. It seemed like a very, very long way up. Angelina was so excited! She couldn't wait to jump on.

"I told you that I don't really like Ferris wheels," whispered Henry timidly.

Angelina tried to reassure him. "Don't worry, Henry,
they're not at all scary," she said gently. "Trust me.
You're going to love it!"

Henry reluctantly followed the others, and up they went, climbing higher and higher.

"Isn't this fun, Henry?" laughed Angelina.

But poor Henry wasn't having fun at all. In fact, he felt quite sick. "I want to get off!" he sobbed loudly.

Angelina was very embarrassed as the huge wheel came to a standstill and an attendant helped them step off the ride.

Henry held William's paw as the four friends lined up for the Haunted House. But Henry still wasn't happy.

"I told you, Angelina! I hate the dark!" he whimpered.

Angelina ignored poor Henry and dragged him inside. There were spooky noises, and it was almost pitch-black! Suddenly, Henry realized that he was no longer holding William's paw. He was all alone!

Henry walked bravely through the darkness until he thought he saw William. Henry reached out his paw. But, oh no! It was a huge, hairy spider.

"Agghhhhh!" screamed Henry.

The lights went on, and Henry looked around him. The
Haunted House didn't seem so scary anymore. He was
very pleased to see Angelina and the others just up ahead.

"I'm scared of spiders," sniffled Henry.

He felt very shy as the attendant led them all out of the
Haunted House. Everyone was watching, and Angelina
looked very cross. Alice and William wandered off,
leaving her with Henry.

"Can I have a blue balloon now?" Henry asked Angelina shyly. "And can I go on the merry-go-round?"

Suddenly, Alice and William rushed up. "You should have come with us, Angelina. We've just been on the swinging boat and the helter-skelter. They were fantastic!"

"It's just not fair," said Angelina.

"You have to come on the Loop-the-Loop roller coaster with us. You just HAVE to!" cried Alice.

"I don't like roller coasters," said Henry.

Angelina sighed.

Suddenly, a clown walked by. "Show starts in ten minutes!" he cried. "Wicky wacky fun for all ages!"

Angelina smiled. "I bet you like clown shows, don't you, Henry?" she said.

At last she was free! She left Henry at the clown show, and soon she, Alice, and William were soaring up high on the roller coaster. They loved it so much that they rode on it SEVEN TIMES!

Henry, meanwhile, wasn't having much fun at the clown show. As his eyes wandered, he saw a big blue balloon float past. He just had to go and catch it!

A little while later, Angelina, Alice, and William arrived at the clown's tent to collect Henry. But Henry wasn't there.

"Henry?" whispered Angelina, her heart beating in her chest. "Where are you?"

The three friends ran through the crowds calling Henry's name. They looked everywhere. Alice even called up to the stilt walker because he could see across the whole fairground. But nobody had seen Henry.

At last they sat down on a bench. Alice tried to comfort Angelina, and William offered her his hankie to blow her nose. "What am I going to do?" cried Angelina.

Suddenly, Angelina saw a blue balloon float past, with Henry running along behind, trying to catch it.

"Henry!" she cried. "Thank goodness!"

Angelina took Henry by the paw, and they set off through the crowds. Angelina even used her precious coins to buy him a big blue balloon.

"Look at the merry-go-round, Angelina!" cried Henry. "I love merry-go-rounds."

Angelina smiled as she helped Henry up onto his favorite ride. "I love merry-go-rounds, too," she said.